BLOOMSBURY
CHILDREN'S BOOKS
LONDON OXFORD NEW YORK NEW DELHI SYDNEY

BLOOMSBURY CHILDREN'S BOOKS
Bloomsbury Publishing Plc
50 Bedford Square, London WC1B 3DP, UK
29 Earlsfort Terrace, Dublin 2, Ireland

BLOOMSBURY, BLOOMSBURY CHILDREN'S BOOKS and the Diana logo
are trademarks of Bloomsbury Publishing Plc

First published in Great Britain in 2023 by Bloomsbury Publishing Plc

A catalogue record for this book is available from the British Library

ISBN: PB: 978-1-5266-2061-3; eBook: 978-1-5266-2062-0

2 4 6 8 10 9 7 5 3 1

Printed and bound in China by C&C Offset Printing Co. Ltd
Shenzhen, Guangdong

NEWS HOUNDS

THE COW CALAMITY

Books by Laura James

Illustrated by Églantine Ceulemans

Captain Pug
Cowboy Pug
Safari Pug
Pirate Pug

Illustrated by Emily Fox

Fabio the World's Greatest Flamingo Detective:
The Case of the Missing Hippo
Fabio the World's Greatest Flamingo Detective:
Mystery on the Ostrich Express
Fabio the World's Greatest Flamingo Detective:
Peril at Lizard Lake

Illustrated by Charlie Alder

News Hounds: The Puppy Problem
News Hounds: The Dinosaur Discovery
News Hounds: The Cow Calamity

For Charles and Rachel – L.J.

For June and Sadie: 'Westies are the besties!' Also for J & W always x – C.A.

Farmer Val was herding the cows into the upper field. Bunty kept a safe distance. She found this the scariest job of all at Withy Hook Farm. There was something about the cows that terrified her. She wasn't sure if it was their swishing tails, their strange mooing or the fact that they could put their tongues up their noses that bothered her most, but she was always glad when the herding was done.

With the last cow safely in the field and tucking into the fresh grass, Bunty nudged the gate with her nose until a satisfying click told her it was shut properly. She then crawled under the gate and into the lane that led back to the farmhouse. It was a relief to be out of the way of those hungry monsters.

As Bunty pondered her dislike of cows, Fliss, Bunty's ever-present fly, hovered greedily over a cowpat. Bunty enjoyed the rare opportunity to return to the farmyard unaccompanied.

One thing Bunty was really good at was predicting the weather. She sniffed the air and lifted her eyes to the sky. Since becoming the weather reporter for the Daily Bark, Bunty took it even more seriously. Every dog in the village depended on her to know when to pester their owners to take them for a walk. Today the weather looked good. Not a cloud in the sky. It was a walk-all-day-if-you-like kind of day.

'Bunty!' Farmer Val called for her. 'Pig time!'

Bunty wagged her tail and followed Farmer Val to the pigsty. She liked the pigs. They were clever animals. Fliss, who loved feeding time, reappeared. She bumped into Bunty's head deliberately. Fliss enjoyed nothing more than bugging Bunty. Bumping into Bunty's head was her favourite way of communicating. Bunty snapped at her, as she often did. She had never actually caught Fliss even though she had tried to many times. Fliss really was a pest.

Farmer Val put the pig feed into the trough. The sow and her piglets tucked in happily, their ears dipping into their food as they ate.

The sound of a van entering the farmyard told Bunty that Stan the postman had arrived. He was early. Bunty eagerly raised the alarm by barking and dancing around Farmer Val's feet. She was keen to make amends for not helping with the cows. Fliss joined in, thinking it was a game, but she sent Bunty off course so that she bumped into Farmer Val, who, in turn, slammed her foot on a rake and landed in the pigswill.

The piglets scattered, squealing. Bunty cowered behind the trough. She had never heard Val cry out like that before.

Stan came rushing over. 'You all right, Val?' he asked the farmer as a piglet oinked in her ear. Stan pulled her to her feet, but she couldn't stand. 'It's my ankle,' she said. 'I must have twisted it as I fell.'

Behind the trough, Fliss flew into Bunty's head repeatedly. Bunty gave her a look that told Fliss to buzz off.

Farmer Val couldn't walk properly, and Stan had to support

her as she hobbled towards the farmhouse. Bunty crept beside them, her tail between her legs.

'It's all right, Bunty,' Farmer Val reassured her. 'I'll be all right.'

But Bunty wasn't so sure.

Once Stan knew the doctor was on the way, he left Farmer Val in the kitchen with her foot up on a stool. Bunty nudged her human's hand in sympathy.

Farmer Val tickled her behind the ear, then sighed. 'What am I going to do now, Bunty? Who's going to look after the farm?'

When the doctor arrived to look after Farmer Val, Bunty slipped out of the house and into the farmyard unnoticed.

She thought of all the jobs that needed doing. The eggs needed collecting from the henhouse, the ewes and their lambs needed to be checked, and Stephen the orphaned lamb would be wanting his bottle soon. The goat pen's fencing was in a terrible state, and the honey had to be extracted from the beehive.

It was quite a list. Fliss sat on Bunty's nose and buzzed insistently. Bunty sighed. 'You're right, Fliss. I'll just have to try my best.' She took a deep breath and set to work.

Farming is a lot harder than it looks, thought Bunty.

The chickens ran out of their coop and Bunty accidentally smashed the eggs.

Stephen wouldn't take his bottle and was very wriggly.

A goat thought Bunty's tail was edible, and the bees were none too happy about her taking their honey.

By the end of the day she'd been kicked, bitten, pecked and stung and she smelt as if she hadn't had a bath since Christmas. Bunty needed help.

The following morning, Gizmo, editor-in-chief of the Daily Bark, was just piecing together an article on the best places to roll in something smelly, when Bunty showed up.

'Goodness, how did you get so many scratches!' Gizmo exclaimed.

'I've got an emergency and I need your help,' replied Bunty.

Gizmo could see Bunty was in a bad way. He patched her up as she told him about the situation at the farm.

'We'll all help, Bunty, don't you worry,' he said. 'Go back to the farm and we'll meet you there.' And as Bunty headed back home, Gizmo set about rounding up the News Hounds.

His first stop was for Jilly, who was just next door. She was delighted to help. 'I love the farm!' she said.

As they walked to the station to pick up Bob, Gizmo confided in Jilly. 'I said I'd help, but I'm not sure I'm really a farm type of dog, Jilly. Perhaps I should stay back and work on the paper.'

'Nonsense, Gizmo,' replied Jilly. 'There'll be something you can do. Besides, you gave her your word.'

‘I know. I’m just not very good with animals,’ he admitted.

On hearing the news about Farmer Val, Bob, the station dog, glanced at the timetable. ‘Colin can handle things for a few hours,’ he said. ‘I’d be happy to help.’

Gizmo and Jilly knew how difficult it was for Bob to leave the running of Puddle Station as the sole responsibility of the stationmaster, so they appreciated the gesture.

They found Lola in Pageant Gardens teaching an exercise class. Her students were so exhausted they were relieved when she ended the session early.

The final stop was the hairdresser in the high street, where Bruno was taking a nap by the front door. He too was happy to help.

'Of course I'll come with you,' he said. 'Ooh, hang on a sec,' he added, popping into the salon and coming out with his grooming bag. 'Just in case any of the animals on the farm are in need of a makeover,' he informed them. 'Like that really big horse. Edward, is it?'

'Edmund,' Jilly corrected him. 'Yeah, he's huge.'

Gizmo gulped. Coming from Jilly, this was saying something.

B

Bunty was delighted when her friends turned up at the farm. Her tail wouldn't stop wagging and even Fliss was positively buzzing.

'There's plenty to do,' she told

them. 'We just have to make sure Farmer Val doesn't see us at work. Now, bark up if there's anything in particular you want to do as I run through the list ... The ewes and their lambs?'

'I can do that,' said Bruno.

'Thank you, Bruno,' said Bunty. 'Who would like to look after the chickens?'

'I can,' replied Bob.

'Excellent, they're over there.'

Bunty pointed her nose in the general direction of the henhouse. 'Who can help me with the fencing for the goats?' she asked next.

'I'll help,' said Lola.

Bunty was pleased with this. She knew Lola could easily outrun a charging billy goat if she needed to.

'That just leaves Jilly and Gizmo ... well, Edmund's stable needs mucking out ...'

Jilly glanced across at Gizmo's

face and saw his look of horror.

‘I can do that,’ she volunteered. ‘We’re probably the same height, after all.’

Gizmo looked very relieved.

‘Gizmo, that just leaves collecting the honey ...’

‘I can do that,’ said Gizmo. His human, Grannie, loved honey on her toast in the morning. He knew all about honey. 'Where is it?' he asked.

'The hives are in the far field,' said Bunty. 'A bit of advice: be careful and don't annoy them.'

'Annoy who?'

But Bunty didn't hear him. She was getting ready to face the cows. She couldn't ask her friends to do such a terrifying task.

Bruno was in his element caring for the sheep. The ewes had been quite stand-offish with Bunty, but it didn't take him long to realise that all they needed was a bit of pampering. He laid his trusty grooming bag on the ground and started work cutting fleeces, shining hoofs and giving shoulder rubs. The new mums felt very relaxed and let him check on their lambs without a fuss.

Bob was doing well with the chickens. He made sure they had enough food and water and carefully gathered their eggs into a basket. Being about the same size as a chicken himself, he found they barely noticed he was there.

Lola did such a good job running away from the charging billy goat that he gave up and had to have a lie-down. This gave her a chance to fix the fencing without being disturbed.

Jilly cleaned out Edmund's stable, gave him some more hay and threw a rug over him.

Meanwhile Bunty slipped through the bars of the upper-field gate unnoticed. She crept towards the cow herd. All she had to do was move them to the lower field, but as she approached she could hear their noisy eating, swishing tails and stomping hoofs. Her heart was in her mouth.

At this exact moment, on the other side of the farm, Gizmo came hurtling towards the farmyard,

barking like he'd never barked before. In hot

pursuit was a very angry swarm of bees.

Gizmo jumped into a nearby water trough to escape attack and the other News Hounds quickly took cover.

In the upper field, Bunty edged closer to the cows. She was determined to overcome her fear. As she crouched down in the long grass, she heard a faint buzzing sound.

'Shh, Fliss!' she whispered.

But the buzzing grew louder.

'Fliss!' she said. 'The cows will hear!' She was almost within kicking distance and getting very nervous.

Fliss bumped into Bunty's head – she really was the most annoying fly – and Bunty flapped her ears in annoyance. But as Fliss landed on her nose, Bunty noticed the buzzing hadn't stopped. In fact, it was getting even louder.

Was Fliss pointing at something?

Bunty turned to look over her shoulder just as the swarm of bees surrounded the cows like a black cloud. Within seconds the cows were in a frenzy, their huge hoofs pounding through the mud away from the bees ... and towards Bunty.

Stampede!

Bunty didn't wait a moment more. She turned tail and ran for the gate.

Back in the farmyard, the News Hounds came out of hiding, and Jilly scooped a bedraggled Gizmo out of the water trough.

'What happened?' she asked.

'Nobody told me there would be bees!' he whined.

'Where did you think honey

came from?' asked Jilly, surprised.

'A shop,' replied Gizmo, 'or, you know, a cupboard.'

Jilly hid her smile as she licked her friend's wounds. 'Mm, you taste like honey!'

'Remember, you're not to eat me, Jilly,' replied Gizmo with a wag of his tail. He was feeling better already.

But just then Bunty ran into the farmyard panting. 'The cows ... the

bees ... they've never done that before!' she exclaimed, trying to catch her breath.

'I'm sorry, Bunty, that was my fault,' confessed Gizmo. 'I think I upset them.'

'Oh. Right. That's OK, Gizmo. Not your fault,' said Bunty. 'But I still haven't moved the cows to the lower field and I need to do it before it rains tomorrow afternoon.'

'We can help you tomorrow morning. Plan Bee,' suggested Bruno with a wink.

'Maybee,' agreed Bob.

'I think I left my Fris-*bee* in the park,' giggled Lola.

'That can't bee,' laughed Jilly.

'Unbeelievable!' exclaimed Gizmo, catching the joke.

Bunty wagged her tail. 'Oh, bee-hive, you lot!'

On their second day of farming, the News Hounds were getting the hang of things a little better and Withy Hook Farm soon looked spick and span.

Bunty decided to give Gizmo an

easy job and asked him to sit outside the stable and be the lookout.

'Are you OK there, Gizmo, keeping an eye out for us?'

'Yes,' replied Gizmo. 'I can do this. It gives me the chance to think up what words I'm going to use for my piece about the farm.'

'If Farmer Val comes anywhere near the window you must bark three times. Got it?' asked Bunty.

'Got it,' replied Gizmo.

'And, Gizmo?'

'Yes?'

'No bees.'

'No bees, Bunty,' he replied.

Bunty wasn't feeling bold enough to try herding the cows again, so she decided to harvest the apples in the orchard instead.

Gizmo's first hour or so of being lookout passed without incident.

The sun was shining, and he sat on the steps outside the stable and took in the new sights, sounds and smells that surrounded him. He was managing to think of lots of pretty words to describe the farm. He felt sure he was going to write his best article yet.

He was just trying to think of a good headline when a large nose appeared over the stable door. Gizmo, sitting on the steps, was at muzzle height with Edmund.

Gizmo felt his heart race, but when Edmund whinnied, his whiskery lips jiggling about, Gizmo's fears left him.

Gizmo glanced over and noticed that the hay feeder was empty.

'Are you hungry, boy?' Gizmo

asked, and without waiting for a reply he jumped down the steps in the only way a dachshund can and climbed on to a nearby stack of hay bales. He tugged on some hay and managed to free a

mouthful, which he carefully offered to Edmund. The horse gently nibbled at it. Gizmo was delighted he was striking up a new friendship and turned round on the bale to get more hay.

But this time, when he tugged on the hay the top bale fell, sending the others crashing. Gizmo dodged out of the way and looked around to see if anyone had noticed. The house was still. He tried to put the hay bale back, but he couldn't move it. It was too big. He tried to shove it with his shoulder. Nothing. He then decided to run at it, but it was like running into a brick wall.

Gizmo thought for a second and decided to go and get something to lever it. He found a shovel which he dragged across from the barn. He pushed it under the bale, but even when he sat on the end of the shovel his weight wasn't enough to budge it.

As he sat there he suddenly remembered he was supposed to be on lookout. He glanced at the farmhouse, and staring right back at him was Farmer Val.

She'd seen everything.

'Woof, woof, woof!'

Every dog followed the drill and froze.

But it was too late.

Bob was
carrying a
basket of eggs,
Bruno was
bottle-feeding
Stephen,
Lola was
herding
up the
ducks and

Jilly was helping Bunty with a barrow full of apples.

Farmer Val picked up the phone.

'Hello, is that *PuddleVision News*? You won't believe the story I've got for you!

In no time Withy Hook farmyard was filled with TV reporters.

Bunty was furious.

Gizmo, being editor-in-chief of the Daily Bark, felt it was his duty to teach the other News Hounds how to deal with the press.

'Remember, this is a "no comment" situation. We don't want the humans knowing about this. Just wag your tail and lick things.'

'Which is my best side?' asked Lola, spinning in circles to look at herself.

'Both are spectacular,' said Bruno, who was a good encourager.

'OK, News Hounds,' Gizmo said. 'It's time for our close-up.'

The camera crews were all very well, but the thing that mattered to Bunty was the farm. Everyone had left their jobs half done.

The door to the chicken coop had been left open and the chickens had started to wander off.

She set about trying to gather them up. Some were in the barn, some in with the pigs, and a little red hen had escaped into the garden and was busy eating vegetables from the vegetable patch.

But worse was to come. She

glanced towards the upper field to see a cow happily strolling through an open gate. To her horror, by the time she reached the field, the last cow was trotting towards Puddle village, the gate swinging on its hinges.

How on earth am I going to get them back? she thought in dismay.

Meanwhile Farmer Val's interview with the TV crew wasn't going well. The people from *PuddleVision News*

didn't seem to believe her.

'So you're saying this big dog here –' the reporter pointed to Jilly – 'wheeled a barrow full of apples?' Jilly tried to look as vacant as possible and went in circles, chasing her own tail.

'And this dog –' the camera panned to Bob, who was scooting on his bottom – 'collects chicken eggs and puts them in a basket?' The reporter gave a snort of laughter.

'Well, you see, I have a bad ankle and the dogs clearly thought I needed help ...'

'Did you take a bump to the head when you hurt your ankle?' asked the reporter.

Farmer Val scratched her head, beginning to doubt herself.

By now Farmer Val's prize cows were scattered around Puddle village.

Bunty sat in the lane by the cows' field in despair. Fliss buzzed and crashed around her head. 'Oh, what shall I do?'

Just then Gizmo panted up the lane towards them.

'Everything all right?' he asked. 'I noticed you'd run off.'

Bunty tilted her head towards the gate. 'They've all gone!' she told him.

'Oh, Bunty!'

'And the worst part

of it is, I'm terrified of cows!'

'Me too!' Gizmo reassured her. 'In fact, most animals frighten me, but I'll help you find them. We'll do this together. And remember, you're much braver than you think – and you know a lot about farming!'

'Thank you, Gizmo,' replied Bunty. 'You're so good with words. Will you walk into the village with me?'

'Of course,' Gizmo said.

Gizmo, Bunty and Fliss made their way to the village. On the way, Bunty came up with a plan.

'I'll round them up,' Bunty told Gizmo when they reached the high street. 'And you stay with them to make sure they don't go missing

again while I find the others.'

Gizmo waited patiently in the middle of Puddle while Bunty went in search of the cows.

The first one was in the dairy section of the village shop. Mr Strange, who ran the village shop, was trembling behind the counter.

OPEN

Bunty felt like doing the same, but knew this was her problem to solve. She decided to take the cow by surprise. Using the mirror in the corner of the shop for guidance, Bunty went down the dried food aisle while the cow moved towards the tinned goods. They met at the corner. 'Moo!' Bunty did her best cow impression. The shock of it sent the cow charging out of the shop.

Bunty yapped and dodged around the cow and, to her utter astonishment, the cow allowed herself to be herded towards where Gizmo was waiting for her.

'There, that's the first one,' Bunty

told Gizmo. 'Just twelve more to go.' She was beginning to feel a little more confident.

Gizmo had chosen a spot in the centre of the high street which had a lovely flower bed and some hanging baskets. The cow started to wrap her tongue around a tasty-looking petunia.

There were three cows by the duck pond, who, with a gentle bit of nudging in the right direction, did as they were told.

The two in the library car park were more stubborn, but moved along nicely when they saw their friends waiting by Gizmo.

A lone cow wandered up to join them of her own accord.

'Now, how many more have I got to find?' Bunty asked Gizmo.

'Another six!' he informed her.

One was in the hairdresser and was being shooed out by Bruno's human. Another had gone into the bookshop, and three more were heading for the car wash at the garage. Bunty sprinted after them and herded them back to Gizmo before they had the full bubble treatment.

One more to find. *Where could she be?* wondered Bunty. Just then a tannoy announcement from the station gave her the answer.

'The next train leaving Platform Two has been delayed due to a cow on the line.'

Bunty rushed over to the track just as the cow sensibly walked over the level crossing.

When Bunty had safely returned her to the herd, Gizmo cheered. 'That's it! Now all we need to do is get them back to the farm.'

Bunty and Gizmo looked at the

feeding cows happily swishing their tails. They tried to move them on but the cows wouldn't budge.

'What are we going to do now?' asked Bunty.

Just then, she realised something strange. For once in her life she was without Fliss. There was no buzzing sound above her head. She looked around.

'Where's Fliss?' Bunty asked Gizmo.

They found Fliss at the back of the herd, buzzing around the head of the biggest cow of all.

'She's pretending to be a swarm of bees!' said Bunty.

She was making more noise than Bunty had ever heard her make before. She even flew up the cow's nose. The cow shook her head in frustration and jostled the cow next to her,

who stumbled out of the way. The cow to her right didn't like this at all, and before they knew it the cows began to stampede straight down the high street in the direction of Withy Hook Farm.

Bunty and Gizmo raced after them, their ears flapping behind their heads they were running so fast. They followed the thunder of hoofs, exhilarated by their triumph.

Just as Farmer Val was trying to answer a particularly difficult question from a news reporter, there was a bellowing from the lane. The camera panned away and focused on the source of the sound.

The team from *PuddleVision News* froze on the spot as the herd thundered towards them.

But at a stern buzz from Fliss the cows took a sharp right and went through the open gate of the lower field. Bunty and Gizmo were right on their heels.

They soon settled back to grazing, and for the first time Bunty didn't feel nervous around them.

'I guess I was just frightened of them because they're so big,' she confessed.

'I felt like that when I first met Jilly,' confided Gizmo.

'Jilly?' asked Bunty, amazed. 'But she's the nicest dog I know.'

'Exactly,' said Gizmo, and as if to

prove his point, a nearby cow gently mooed in Bunty's ear, which made them laugh.

Gizmo headed back to the farmyard as Bunty shut the gate with the familiar, satisfying click. As she counted the herd one last time, Fliss landed on her paw.

'Thank you,' she said to Fliss, who did a loop the loop and buzzed playfully around Bunty's head.

'We make a great team, you and I,' said Bunty.

'Did you get that?' the reporter asked her cameraman. He nodded.

'You're live in five,' her producer

told her, and on his nod the reporter spoke directly to the camera.

'We're here at Withy Hook Farm witnessing, we think you'll agree, the most extraordinary phenomenon. On this small farm, where the farmer has been sick and unable to work, it is the dogs that have taken on the workload. I have to confess, I was sceptical at first, but wait till you see this ...'

They ran the footage of Bunty and Gizmo herding the cows into the lower field.

'And as you can see, this dog – Bunty – even knows how to shut a gate. And look at her friend, Cosmo, I think his name is. Isn't he cute?'

At that point it started to rain.

Once the camera crew had left, all Farmer Val's friends dropped by to congratulate her on her television appearance.

'It's quite embarrassing really,' she told everyone. 'I was sure I'd seen the dogs doing farm work, but I must have taken a knock to my head when I fell in the pigs' breakfast. Thank goodness Bunty shut the gate like she did – it made her look like a real farmer. It's a little trick I taught her. Of course, she didn't really herd the cows. She hates cows!'

Gizmo didn't really mind the TV crew getting his name wrong. They clearly weren't proper journalists.

'Do you think I'm cute?' he asked Bunty.

'Beeautiful!' replied Bunty, and Fliss agreed, buzzing loudly in a way that made Gizmo's stings itch.

He was more than happy to hand the farm work back to Farmer Val, Bunty and Fliss. Besides, he had the real story to write up in the Daily Bark.

THE
END

Look out for

OUT NOW!

Turn the page for a sneak peek

Gizmo was a city dog. A prince of the urban jungle. His paths were clear, and his lawns were mown. He and Grannie owned the streets they ...

GRANNIE MAKES SURPRISE MOVE TO THE COUNTRY TO WRITE MEMOIRS! GIZMO SHOCKED!

Gizmo worried as he and Grannie drove away from the only home he'd ever known. They were going to a place called Puddle. That didn't sound good – he hated getting his paws wet. But where Grannie went, he went.

Gizmo had finally managed to nap, when a bump in the road woke him. They'd arrived. He sniffed the air. It smelt … different. Too clean.

His worry deepened.

As Grannie made her way to the house, Gizmo explored the garden. It seemed very strange to him. For a start there wasn't a smartly dressed park attendant.

There were no fountains, no rows of benches, and where were the rubbish bins? To him it seemed wild and unruly. He was carefully edging his way around a flower bed when he heard a voice.

'Hello there!'

Was it the great dog in the sky?

'Over here!' said the voice.

Gizmo looked all around but he couldn't see anyone. Ahead of him was a white fence with a small hole in it. He peered through. More wilderness. All he could see were shrubs and bushes and four strange hairy tree trunks.

'Is there anybody there?' he asked.

'Yes, me!' came the reply.

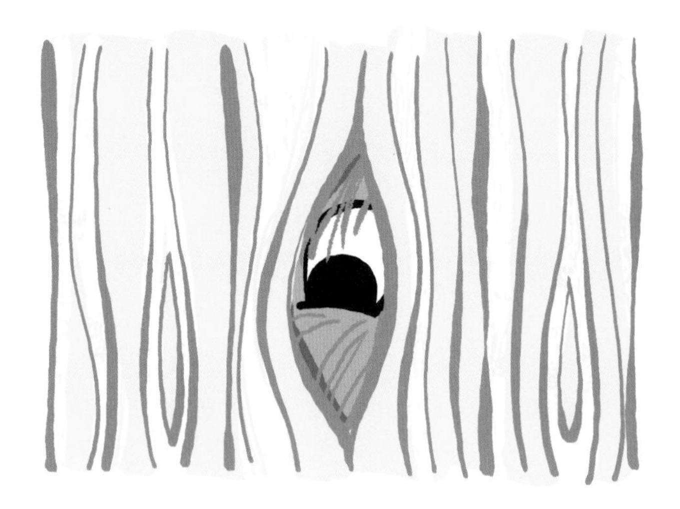

Suddenly his gaze was met by an enormous eye. He jumped back, startled, and the eye blinked.

'I'm Jilly,' it said. 'Pleased to meet you.'

Gizmo tried to wag his tail in a friendly way, but he was shaking.

'Um, hello,' he replied. 'I'm Gizmo. I've never met an enormous eye before.'

'Up here,' insisted the voice. 'At the top of the fence.'

Gizmo craned his head back as far as he could and saw the biggest, furriest face he'd ever seen. He recognised the eye.

'What are you?' he asked, amazed.

'I'm an Irish wolfhound!'

'What are you standing on?' Gizmo asked. He couldn't work out how she could be looking over the fence when it was so high.

'Nothing,' said Jilly, confused.

Gizmo looked back through the hole in the fence and realised that what he'd thought were tree trunks were in fact Jilly's very long legs. She was the biggest dog he'd ever seen! He took a nervous step back.

'What are *you*?' Jilly asked.

'I'm a dachshund,' Gizmo replied. Despite his nerves he couldn't help showing off his long, smooth body. 'Or a sausage dog. It's easier to say.'

And have you read
the second story about the News Hounds

PAWfect for anyone who's ever wondered
what their dog does when they're not looking!

AVAILABLE NOW

Read all Fabio's adventures

Available now

About the Author and Illustrator

LAURA JAMES has two writing companions, her wire-haired dachshunds, Brian and Florence. They are a constant source of inspiration for her stories and she adores their every bark, tail-wag, and tummy-rub request. Sometimes she wonders if they might secretly be writing about her too!

CHARLIE ALDER lives in Devon, England, with her husband and son. When not drawing chickens or dogs, Charlie can be found in her studio drinking coffee, arranging her crayons and inventing more accidental animal heroes.